SAILING HOME

A STORY OF A CHILDHOOD AT SEA

Told by Gloria Rand · Illustrated by Ted Rand

A Cheshire Studio Book

NorthSouth
BOOKS

NEW YORK · LONDON

OURS WAS A WONDERFUL CHILDHOOD, a childhood spent at sea.
My sister Dagmar, my brother, Albert, and I, Matilda, grew up aboard the
John Ena, a four-masted sailing bark that carried cargo all over the world.

Our father was the ship's captain; the ship was our home. Only when the cargo was coal, which is highly inflammable, did we have to live ashore.

The *John Ena* had bedrooms, a bathroom, and a main saloon that was a combination living room with a pink marble fireplace and a dining room with a big round table. There was a kitchen called the galley and a storage room full of everything we needed.

Unlike most homes, ours didn't stay put. At night, the ship kept moving, so every morning we woke up far away from where we'd gone to sleep.

It often seemed as if we lived on a farm, not a ship. Roosters crowed, hens clucked, and ducks quacked. Mother raised them all in neat pens below deck, so we'd have fresh meat and eggs to add to the ship's food supply. Dagmar and I collected the eggs.

We all took turns caring for our pets as we traveled around the world. There was Minnie the cat and a dog named Murphy. We had a mongoose, a monkey, a pig, and even a kangaroo.

The day the kangaroo accidentally jumped overboard we screamed for help. The crew quickly lowered a life boat and rescued it.

Our pet pig wasn't so lucky. She fell into a pot of hot tar the men were using to repair the ship's deck. Piggy died. We had a real funeral for her and a dignified burial at sea.

Instead of a backyard or a playground we had a great wooden deck where we played tag, hide-and-seek, and catch, always with beanbags, because balls bounced overboard. We swung on rope swings and, after our baby sister Ena was born, we took turns wheeling her around the deck in a baby buggy.

When the winds were blowing hard and the sea was full of big waves, we played inside. Our favorite game was sliding across the main saloon floor in cardboard boxes, crashing into one another as the ship rolled from side to side.

"Time to calm down," Mother would say softly when we got rowdy. "Let's read for a while."

Mother taught us how to read and count. She was a good teacher. Father was a good teacher, too.

"Name that planet," he'd say, pointing to a bright steady light in the dark night sky. Before long we could tell planets from stars and even understood about celestial navigation. As a special treat Father gave us our own set of signaling flags, and we learned to send messages. From the stern of the ship we sent messages to Father at the bow, and he signaled messages back to us.

There were no radios then, and when we were out at sea we seldom saw another ship. If a ship did pass close enough for us to see each other clearly, Father or one of the crew exchanged greetings and information, using signaling flags.

Real school began when Miss Shipman, a governess, came aboard as our teacher. Albert didn't like her at all. Dagmar said she looked mean, but I thought she was nice.

With Miss Shipman in charge, we went to school at the dining table six days a week, mornings and afternoons, with only an hour off for lunch and no recesses.

Miss Shipman was good at teaching us history, science, mathematics, and languages. But teaching us geography was impossible for her. We'd seen so much of the world, we knew more than she did. We'd tell her about our family picnics in Japan and all about palaces and cathedrals we had visited in Europe. Miss Shipman was impressed, but not with Albert.

Albert didn't like school. He played hooky a
lot. He'd sneak off to mend sails with the ship's
carpenter or help the crew scrub down the
deck with flat stones called holy stones.
Sometimes Albert crawled up and hid in
a little cubbyhole by the masthead. Miss
Shipman would tattle to Father, and
Father would bring Albert back to
school.

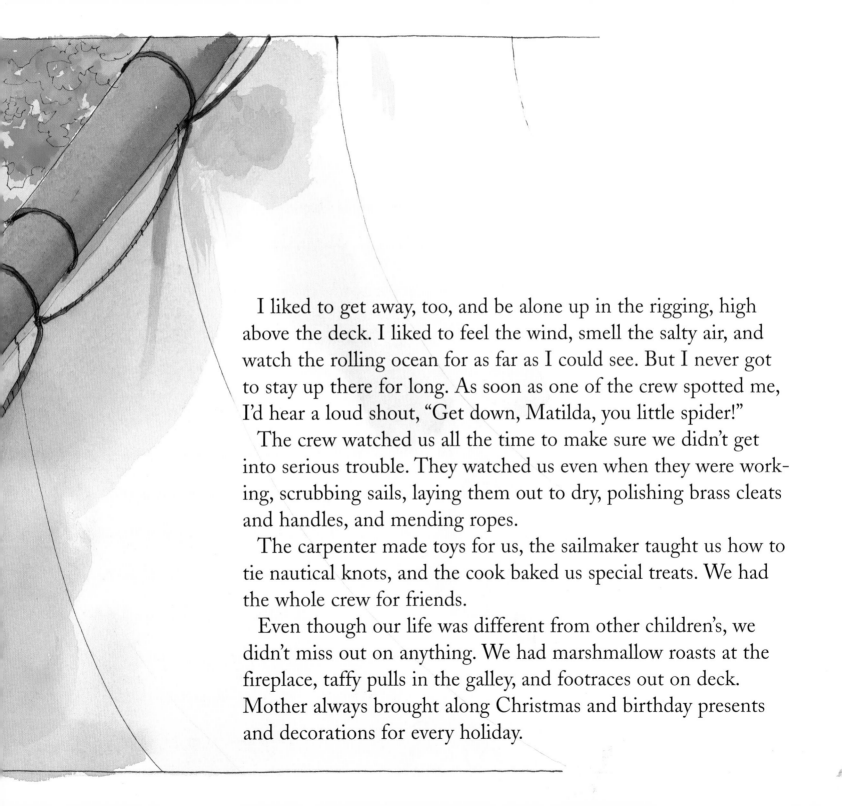

I liked to get away, too, and be alone up in the rigging, high above the deck. I liked to feel the wind, smell the salty air, and watch the rolling ocean for as far as I could see. But I never got to stay up there for long. As soon as one of the crew spotted me, I'd hear a loud shout, "Get down, Matilda, you little spider!"

The crew watched us all the time to make sure we didn't get into serious trouble. They watched us even when they were working, scrubbing sails, laying them out to dry, polishing brass cleats and handles, and mending ropes.

The carpenter made toys for us, the sailmaker taught us how to tie nautical knots, and the cook baked us special treats. We had the whole crew for friends.

Even though our life was different from other children's, we didn't miss out on anything. We had marshmallow roasts at the fireplace, taffy pulls in the galley, and footraces out on deck. Mother always brought along Christmas and birthday presents and decorations for every holiday.

Only once, when I was ten, we almost didn't have Christmas.

That year, as we crossed the China Sea, the weather turned wild. We had just started to put up red and green garlands and ropes of sparkling tinsel when Father rushed in.

"Here, grab this end, and tie up that chair," Father ordered as he unwound a big coil of heavy line.

We all knew what to do. Like experts we tied the piano and all the furniture to the railing that ran along the walls of the main saloon and to big hooks the carpenter was screwing into the floor. Mother put little things, lamps, knickknacks, and our candy dish into a heavy sea chest. Everything had to be tied up or put away, otherwise, when the ship pitched and rolled, there would have been stuff crashing and flying all over the place.

It wasn't long before we were in the middle of a terrible
storm that stayed with us for days. The sky was black. There
were huge bolts of lightning, and thunder roared so loud you
could hardly think.

No matter how bad the storm became, Miss Shipman made
us go to school. The seas got so rough it wasn't safe to sit at
the dining table, so we all sat on the floor while Miss Shipman
conducted class. We slid back and forth across the floor as the
ship rode the waves. It was like riding a roller coaster.

After school we pressed our faces against the portholes and cheered as tons of water smashed against the glass. When Mother saw what we were doing she pulled us back.

"I don't want you to get hurt," she said. "Those waves could shatter the glass."

Two of the crew did get hurt when a gigantic wave swept them down the length of the ship. Father dashed out and pulled them to safety. Mother sewed up their bad cuts with ordinary needle and thread. One of the sailors cried.

The storm got worse and worse. Lifeboats were torn loose and smashed into pieces by gigantic waves, and the sails were ripped to shreds by screaming winds. But lucky for us we didn't get seasick. We never did. Father decided the safest place for all of us to be was on the floor of the ship's chart room. That's when we began to get scared. Father tried to get us to think about something else, like having a Christmas party.

"When we get through this storm," he promised, "we're going to have a grand holiday celebration. It will be the most wonderful party we've ever had. Let's start planning it now."

At that moment the ship rolled onto her side and didn't roll back. We all clung together.

"Mary," he said as he kissed our mother, "the ship has broached, and I think we're about to sink."

"Yes, dear," said Mother, looking Father right in the eye and smiling the bravest smile you'd ever hope to see.

Neither of them showed any panic or fear, and that made us children feel brave, too. Father kissed each of us and told us we were great sailors.

It seemed our family stayed hugging together forever, then the *John Ena* quivered a strange quiver and slowly righted herself!

Gradually, the storm ended, and the sea became calm.

"Time to get our celebration ready," said Father. He had never sounded so happy.

With all of us helping, everything was soon put back where it belonged.

"Girls, hang all this ribbon and tinsel up everywhere. And Albert, you're in charge of decorating the wooden Christmas tree, the one the carpenter made for us." Mother was excited.

"Don't look, I'm about to bring out the presents. Your father has a surprise for you, too, don't you, dear?"

We all laughed because we knew what Father's surprise always was at Christmas. He became Santa.

That night we dressed up in our party clothes. The crew sang "My Bonnie Lies Over the Ocean." They sang the best they had ever sung. The cook filled the table with delicious treats, and we played the gramophone and clapped and cheered watching Father dance with Mother. They were such good dancers.

As promised, it was the best Christmas ever.
We were safe, right where we loved to be.
We were at home, home on the sea.

PICTURES FROM A LIFE AT SEA

CLOCKWISE FROM TOP LEFT:
Captain Mads Albert Madsen; the *John Ena*
under full sail; Anna Marie Madsen; Albert,
Dagmar, and Matilda sitting on the ship's
anchor; Dagmar, Albert, and Matilda on
deck; baby Ena in a wicker carriage with
diapers drying in the wind behind her;
Matilda in her rope swing.

AFTERWORD

This story is based on a real family's life aboard a four-masted sailing bark, the *John Ena*, one of many sailing ships that carried cargo all over the world in the 1800s. Named for an important Chinese-Hawaiian merchant, the magnificent *John Ena* was 312 feet 9 inches long and 48 feet wide. She carried coal, lumber, sugar, barley, wheat, and general cargo to ports around the world.

She made forty-four voyages between 1896 and 1910 under the command of Captain Mads Albert Madsen, some only a few weeks long, others nearly five months. On most of these voyages, Captain Madsen was accompanied by his wife, Anna Marie, and their children, Matilda, Albert, Dagmar, and Ena. Two of the children, Albert and Dagmar, were born aboard.

"When do we sail?" the children would ask their parents whenever the *John Ena* was in port. "When are we going back out to sea?"

Out at sea was where they most wanted to be. On the few occasions when these young sailors lived ashore they described school as a nightmare, even though they did well and easily made friends with the other children.

Their life aboard ship was luxurious, as family life was on many tall ships. Linen tablecloths and napkins were standard at their table. Food was served on heavy white ironstone ware, decorated with a deep blue band and inscribed with the *John Ena* insignia. Furnishings were plush and would have been acceptable in any mansion ashore.

When faster, more efficient steamships took over trade and passenger routes, Captain Madsen became a qualified steamship captain. Quarters aboard these ships did not offer the same spacious accommodations for family living as had the large sailing ships. The Madsens settled in Honolulu, Hawaii.

Their walk down the *John Ena*'s gangplank for the last time was heartbreaking for each member of the Madsen family. The captain was the last to leave. With baby Ena in his arms and tears in his eyes, he turned as he stepped onto the dock and saluted his ship. Then he saluted his crew.

"Aloha, Captain, good luck." The crew was heart-broken, too.

All four children married and continued to live in the Hawaiian Islands. Before Anna Marie died at the age of fifty-seven, there were three grand-children. Two more grandchildren were born before Captain Mads Albert Madsen died at the age of eighty-seven.

Captain Madsen and his daughter, Ena Atlanta Sroat, collaborated on a journal that covered the years the Madsens made their home aboard the *John Ena*. The captain's granddaughter Ena Marie Sroat graciously made this journal available to the Rands. Further research at the Port Townsend, Washington, Library; the Seattle Museum of History and Industry; the San Francisco Maritime National Historical Park; and San Francisco's J. Porter Shaw Library helped authenticate the illus-trations.

It is with great pleasure that Gloria and Ted Rand offer today's children the story, told in words and pictures, of a happy, courageous family and their life at sea.

Dedicated to the memory of an exceptional family—Captain Mads Albert Madsen, his wife, Anna Marie, and their four children, Matilda, Albert, Dagmar, and Ena.

Special thanks to Andrew Price for bringing this story to our attention, and to Ena Marie Sroat, granddaughter of Captain and Mrs. Madsen, for sharing her family's fascinating history.

PHOTO CREDITS: Photo of the *John Ena* courtesy of the San Francisco Maritime NHP Collection (photo J7.3059n) of the San Francisco Maritime National Historic Park, San Francisco, California. Photos of Captain Madsen and his wife from the collection of the Jefferson County Historical Society, Port Townsend, Washington. All other photos courtesy of Ena Marie Sroat.

Published in the United States by North-South Books Inc., New York, in 2001. Published simultaneously in Canada by North-South Books Inc., an imprint of NordSüd Verlag AG, Gossau Zürich, Switzerland. First paperback edition published in 2006 by North-South Books Inc. Distributed in the United States by North-South Books Inc., New York. Library of Congress Cataloging-in-Publication Data is available.
ISBN-13: 978-0-7358-2079-1 / ISBN-10: 0-7358-2079-1
(paperback edition) 10 9 8 7 6 5 4 3 2 1
Printed in Belgium